This book
belongs to

....

My First BOOK of Princess Stories

Compiled by Catherine Veitch

Miles
KeLLY

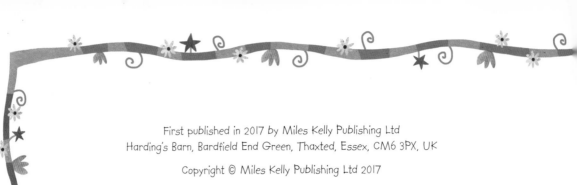

First published in 2017 by Miles Kelly Publishing Ltd
Harding's Barn, Bardfield End Green, Thaxted, Essex, CM6 3PX, UK

2 4 6 8 10 9 7 5 3 1

Publishing Director Belinda Gallagher
Creative Director Jo Cowan
Editorial Director Rosie Neave
Design Manager Simon Lee
Image Manager Liberty Newton
Production Elizabeth Collins, Caroline Kelly
Reprographics Stephan Davis, Jennifer Cozens

ISBN 978-1-78617-238-9

Printed in China

British Library Cataloguing-in-Publication Data
A catalogue record for this book is available from the British Library

Acknowledgements

The publishers would like to thank the following artists who have contributed to this book:

Cover and decorative frames: Maddie Frost (The Bright Agency)

Advocate Art: Natalia Moore

The Bright Agency: Maddie Frost, Maxine Lee, Sarah Jennings, Clair Rossiter, Louise Wright

All other artwork from the Miles Kelly Artwork Bank

Made with paper from a sustainable forest

www.mileskelly.net

Contents

ALL'S WELL THAT ENDS WELL

7

Cinderella

There was once a rich man whose wife had died and left him with a young daughter. His daughter grew up to be good and kind.

Eventually, the rich man

married again. His new wife had two daughters who were mean to the rich man's daughter. They took away her pretty dresses and made her wear old, worn clothes and work in the kitchen.

ALL'S WELL THAT ENDS WELL

They forced her to get up early to fetch wood to make the fire, and to wash all their clothes. At night, the sisters made her sleep by the fire in the coal dust, and because she was always so dusty with cinders they called her Cinderella.

One day a messenger came with an invitation from the King. There was going to be a grand ball over three days. The ball

Cinderella

was for the prince, and all the
ladies in the land were invited.
The prince would choose a lady
to marry at the end of the
three days. The stepsisters
were so excited! The ball was to
start that evening, so they
ordered Cinderella to help them
get ready.

"Comb our hair, clean our
shoes and button our dresses!"
they shouted at poor Cinderella.

ALL'S WELL THAT ENDS WELL

At last, Cinderella's stepmother and sisters left for the ball, leaving her alone with lots of housework to do. Poor Cinderella went outside and sat down by a tree and cried. It was so unfair that her stepsisters could go to the ball when she had chores to do.

Suddenly there was a flash and a white dove flew down from a tree. It was carrying

Cinderella

the most beautiful gold dress,
and twinkling, sparkly shoes.
Cinderella put them on
and was whisked off
to the ball.

The prince spotted
Cinderella at once and
asked her to dance.
They danced
together all evening.
But Cinderella
knew she had to

13

be home before her stepmother
and sisters. So she slipped
away when the prince wasn't
looking and ran all the way
home. The poor prince wondered
where Cinderella had gone.

On the second day of the
ball, after her stepmother and
sisters had left, Cinderella sat
by the tree again and the same
thing happened. The dove
brought her the most beautiful

dress and shoes and whisked her off to the ball. The prince was waiting for Cinderella, and again he danced with her all night. Once more, as it grew late, Cinderella slipped away and hurried home.

When her stepmother and sisters returned, they talked about the beautiful princess who had danced with the prince all night. They didn't know that the princess was really Cinderella.

On the third day when her stepmother and sisters had gone to the ball, Cinderella again went outside to sit by the tree. This time the dove brought her an even more beautiful dress and shoes, and again the prince danced with her all evening.

But when Cinderella slipped away at the end of the night, one of her sparkly shoes came off her foot. The prince picked up the shoe and said, "I will marry the lady whose foot fits perfectly into this shoe."

The next morning the prince asked all the ladies of the land to come to the palace and try on the shoe. Cinderella's stepsisters pushed their way into the room where the shoe was. One at a time, they squeezed their big, clumsy feet into the little shoe but it was clear that it didn't fit. Cinderella came to the palace in her dirty clothes. Her stepsisters laughed

at the thought of the shoe fitting her, but Cinderella's little foot slipped into the shoe perfectly. The prince looked at Cinderella's face and knew that this was the beautiful lady he had danced with at the ball.

"This is my bride," he cried. They were married the following day and lived happily ever after.

19

The Goose Girl

Once upon a time there was a beautiful princess. When the princess grew up she was expected to marry a prince who lived in a faraway land. So the princess set off for the prince's palace with her maid. She rode upon a talking horse called Falada, which was given to her by a good fairy.

On the way, the princess became thirsty so she asked her maid for a drink. But the maid replied, "Get it yourself!" The princess was surprised and a little afraid. They rode on, but the sun was so hot that the princess was soon thirsty again.

ALL'S WELL THAT ENDS WELL

Once more the princess asked her maid for a drink, but again she refused to get one.

Then the maid said, "I will ride Falada and you will ride my horse." The princess was too scared to say no. She also had to give the maid her royal clothes, and put on the maid's dirty clothes.

At last they

reached the prince's palace, and the maid said she would make sure the princess went to prison if she told anyone what had happened. But Falada had seen everything.

The prince was happy to see the princess – he didn't know that it was the maid dressed in the princess's clothes. The real princess was sent to look after the king's geese with a boy called Conrad.

The maid was worried that Falada would tell the prince she wasn't really the princess. So she said to him, "The horse I rode here was very wild, I want you to cut off its head." The prince was shocked but he didn't want to upset her. So poor Falada was killed and her head nailed to a gate. The real princess wept when she heard what had happened.

The next day, the real princess and Conrad passed through the gate beneath Falada's head. The princess cried, "Oh Falada! Look at your head on that gate!"

And the head replied, "Dear princess, if your mother knew what had happened her heart would be *broken.*"

Conrad and the princess took the geese into a field, and the princess stopped to comb her hair. Conrad wanted a strand of her lovely hair but the princess

said, "Blow wind, blow! Blow
Conrad's hat! Go!" At once a
gust of wind blew Conrad's hat
away and he had to chase after
it. When he returned, the
princess had tied her hair back,
and Conrad was angry and
would not speak to her.

The next day the same thing
happened, and the day after
that. At the end of the third
day, Conrad spoke to the king.

"I cannot look after the geese with that strange girl any more as she does nothing but tease me." Conrad told the King what happened, but the King told him to go out again the following day.

This time the King hid behind the gate. He heard what the real princess said to Falada's head, and what the head replied. He saw how the princess's hair glittered in the sun, and he heard the princess tell the wind to blow Conrad's hat away. When the goose girl returned that evening the King asked her why she said those things to the horse's head.

"I shall be killed if I tell you," she wept. But the King begged her to tell him the truth, so she told him the whole story.

The King was very angry

when he heard what had
happened. He told his
servants to bring the
princess her royal
clothes. She looked
beautiful! Then he
told his son that
the lady he thought
was a princess was
really a maid.
The maid was
sent far away

30

and the prince fell in love with the real princess, and they were married. The good fairy visited and brought Falada back to life, and the prince, princess and Falada lived happily ever after.

The Story of Princess Haya

When Princess Haya was little, her mother died and her father remarried. His new wife was mean to Princess Haya saying, "You are not my child!" But Haya was good and kind.

One day the Emperor of Japan visited Princess Haya's home. He asked Haya and her stepmother to play him some music. Princess Haya had worked hard learning her music, but her stepmother was lazy and hadn't practised much. Haya played beautifully, but her stepmother kept forgetting the notes. The Emperor was not pleased with the stepmother, but he gave Haya gifts for playing so well.

This made the stepmother angry. She wanted to get rid of Haya, so she bought some poison. Then she carefully poured two glasses of orange juice, one for her son and one for Haya. She put the poison in one glass. However, she muddled up the glasses and gave the poisoned drink to her son by mistake. Suddenly the boy screamed and dropped to the floor. The wicked stepmother blamed Haya for this and hated her even more.

When Princess Haya was thirteen, her beautiful singing was spoken about across the land. At this time it rained so much that many of the fields were flooded. The Emperor hated hearing the drumming sound of the rain and became ill with worry. He asked Princess Haya to sing for him at his palace to make him feel better.

So Haya sang before the Emperor. Throughout the palace, people listened to her sweet-sounding voice. Immediately, the rain stopped and the water ran

off the fields and they were no longer flooded. The Emperor felt much better and everyone was pleased with Princess Haya.

The only person who wasn't happy was Haya's mean stepmother. She told a servant to take Haya into the mountains and leave her there. So the servant took Haya, but he felt sorry for her. He built a cottage, and lived there with his wife and

Princess Haya.

Haya's father was desperate to find his missing daughter, and he looked everywhere for her. One day he was out hunting in the mountains and came across a cottage. Princess Haya was in the garden singing, and when her father heard her beautiful voice he knew at once that it was his long-lost daughter.

"Dearest Haya!" he cried.

ALL'S WELL THAT ENDS WELL

When Haya saw her father she ran into his arms. She told him everything that her stepmother had done to her.

When her stepmother heard that Haya had been found, she ran away and was never heard of

40

again. Princess Haya lived happily with her father. A few years later she married a handsome prince, and she became a kind and clever ruler.

The Red Slippers

Rosy-red was a sweet little girl, with beautiful brown eyes, soft pink cheeks and dark hair. Sadly her mother died the day she was born so Rosy-red was cared for by her

The Red Slippers

grandmother, who loved her dearly. On her first birthday Rosy-red's father gave her some red slippers. As Rosy-red's feet grew, her red slippers got bigger too, so they always fitted her. No one knew that the slippers were magic.

One day when Rosy-red returned home from a walk in the woods, she found that her grandmother had gone. In the

house were three strangers.
"Who are you?" asked
Rosy-Red.

The Red Slippers

"I am your new mother," said one, "and these are your new sisters." Rosy-red's father had married again and his new wife had sent her grandmother away.

Rosy-red's new mother was mean to her. She made her fetch water from the well and carry the heavy bucket all the way home. Her sisters often shouted at her too. Rosy-red was sad, so she didn't wear her red slippers anymore.

Then one day, as Rosy-red lowered the bucket into the well, she sang, "Swing and sweep and don't stop until you come back up to the top."

A genie was sleeping at the bottom of the well and Rosy-red's song woke him. The genie loved her sweet song so much that he dropped some precious jewels into the bucket.

The Red Slippers

Rosy-red thought, 'If I give these jewels to my sisters maybe they will be kinder to me.' So she handed the jewels to her sisters and told them all about what happened at the well. But the sisters weren't happy, and they snatched the jewels and the bucket from Rosy-red.

The sisters ran to the well and as they lowered the bucket

they sang Rosy-red's song. But the genie didn't like their croaky voices, so he filled their bucket with toads and frogs.

The sisters were angry and threw Rosy-red out of the house. She just had time to put on her red

48

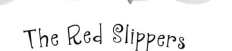

slippers, then she ran away into the woods.

After a while it began to get dark and Rosy-red was frightened. She saw a light in a cave, and an old woman invited her inside. It was Rosy-red's grandmother!

Rosy-red was so tired that she soon fell asleep. When she awoke, she found that one of her red slippers was missing. "I must go and look for it," said Rosy-Red.

"You can't do that, a storm is raging," said her grandmother. So Rosy-red went back to sleep.

A little while later, Rosy-red was woken by a man's voice. The man had found a red slipper and he asked Rosy-red's grandmother if she knew who it belonged to. But grandmother

The Red Slippers

was afraid that Rosy-red's
stepsisters had sent him to find
her. So she said she didn't
know, and the strange man left.

The next day the man called
again. He said, "I am a prince. I
must find who this shoe belongs
to." So Rosy-red bravely
stepped out of her hiding place.
She was wearing her one red
slipper. The prince put the other
red slipper on Rosy-red's bare

ALL'S WELL THAT ENDS WELL

foot. "Let us get to know each other. If you like me, we will get married and you will be my princess," said the prince.

The Red Slippers

So Rosy-red left the cave with her grandmother and the prince. She spent many happy days living in the prince's palace and soon they were married. And from then on she always wore her magical red slippers.

Princess Rosette

Once upon a time there lived a king and a queen who had two handsome sons and a beautiful baby daughter.

When it was time to christen their daughter Rosette, they

invited the fairies. The queen asked them what would happen in her daughter's life. But the fairies didn't have good news.

"Because of her, Rosette's brothers will have bad luck."

The king and queen were worried about their sons. So they kept Rosette in a tower to stop her bringing any bad luck to their sons.

Many years later when the

king and queen died, the eldest son let Rosette out of tower. The first thing she did was walk in the palace gardens, and she was amazed by the colourful flowers growing there. She came across a

Princess Rosette

beautiful peacock
and said, "I will
marry the King
of the peacocks."
Her brothers
laughed at her for
saying she would
marry a peacock!
But the princes
loved their sister,
so they went in
search of the King

57

of the peacocks. After many
weeks they found him! The
princes showed the King a
picture of their sister.

"She is the most beautiful
princess in the world," the King
said. So Rosette's brothers
asked if he would marry her,
and he said he would if she was
as beautiful as her picture. But
if she wasn't, then he would cut
off the princes' heads! Then the

princes were put in prison until Rosette arrived.

The princess set off in a boat to the kingdom of the peacocks. She took her little dog named Frisk with her, and a maid. But not long into the journey the maid had a wicked plan. When the princess was asleep she threw her bed, with the princess and Frisk still on it, into the sea. When the princess awoke she was terrified to find herself floating out to sea. She held on tight to the bed, with Frisk sitting behind her.

Meanwhile the maid dressed in the princess's clothes. She met the king of the peacocks

and pretended that she was Princess Rosette. But the maid was not as beautiful as the princess, and when the King saw this, he was angry, as he thought the princes had tried to play a trick on him.

The princes were brought before the King to explain themselves. He wanted to chop off their heads, but the princes said, "Please give us some time to prove to you that we are telling the truth."

Meanwhile, an old man had rescued Princess Rosette and Frisk from the sea. As the princess was feeling hungry, she tied a basket to Frisk and told him to bring back some food from the best kitchen he could find. Of course the best kitchen belonged to the King of peacocks.

ALL'S WELL THAT ENDS WELL

So the little dog
ran all the way to
the king's kitchen

Princess Rosette

and stole his food. This
happened again and again, until
the cook followed the little dog
to the old man's cottage. Then
he ran back to the king
and told him where all
his dinners had gone.
The king said he

would like to go and see for himself who was stealing his food, so he went to the old man's cottage. He arrived just in time to see the princess and the old man finishing his dinner.

The princess told the king everything that had happened. The king realized that she was was the real Princess Rosette, and that the princes were telling the truth. Rosette was indeed as beautiful as her picture and the king fell in love with her. The princes were let out of prison, and Rosette and the king of peacocks were married.

Sleeping Beauty

Once upon a time in a faraway land, a King and queen had a beautiful baby girl. They arranged a feast and invited many guests to celebrate the baby's arrival. The queen said, "I will invite the fairies, too, so they will be kind to our little daughter." So they invited twelve fairies but they didn't ask the thirteenth fairy because she was so mean.

After the feast, the fairies stood around the baby princess's cradle. Each fairy waved her wand and gave a special gift to the princess, such as goodness, kindness and

ALL'S WELL THAT ENDS WELL

happiness. Suddenly, just before
the last fairy was about to give
her gift, the door burst
open. It was
the thirteenth

fairy. She was angry because she hadn't been invited, and she went up to the baby and said, "When the princess is fifteen she will prick her finger on a spindle and die!"

The king and queen were very upset when they heard this, and the mean fairy flew off. But everyone had forgotten that the last fairy had still to give her gift. She stepped forward and said, "I cannot take away the bad wish, but I can change it."

So the last fairy said that when the princess pricked her finger she would not die, but would instead fall asleep for one hundred years. All the people in the palace would fall asleep, too. So when the princess woke up, her family and friends would all be there too.

The princess grew up to be good, kind and happy, all of the things that the fairies had said she would be. But on the day of her fifteenth birthday, the princess decided to explore an old part of the palace. She found a door that she hadn't seen before, with a gold key in the lock. The princess turned the key and slowly the door creaked open.

ALL'S WELL THAT ENDS WELL

Inside the room sat an old woman, who was spinning wool. The old lady was really the mean fairy in disguise. The princess asked, "What are you doing?" And as she did so, she touched the spindle and pricked her finger.

74

Sleeping Beauty

At once, the princess fell into
a deep sleep. And just as the
fairy had wished, the king,
queen and everyone else in the
palace fell asleep, too.

Over many years, a thorny
hedge grew all around the
palace. It grew so thick
and high that soon
no part of the
palace could
be seen.

People forgot that it was there.
Then one day, exactly one
hundred years later, a prince
was riding by. He caught a
glimpse of the palace and used
an axe to chop his way through
the thorny hedge. The palace
was dusty and covered in
cobwebs and there were people
sleeping everywhere. Even the
pigeons on the roof had their
heads tucked under their wings.

The prince walked further until he came to the door with the golden key. He turned the key and found the princess sleeping inside. She looked so beautiful that the prince bent down and kissed her.

At that moment, the spell was broken and the princess opened her eyes. The prince and princess fell in love at first sight. Then everyone in the palace woke up. The pigeons lifted their heads from under their wings, the horses shook themselves, and the dogs jumped up and barked.

The prince and princess went in search of the king and queen to ask if they could get married. Of course the king and queen agreed, and a week later the wedding took place. Everyone came to the wedding, including the fairies. But of course the bad fairy wasn't invited!

79

BRAVE AND BOLD

The Secret Princess

Once upon a time there was a prince and princess who were happily married. But the prince decided to explore some faraway lands. So he said goodbye to his wife and set off on his travels. He visited many lands and had lots of adventures, but eventually was taken prisoner by a mean King.

The prince sent a message to his wife saying, "Sell our palace, then come and rescue me from this prison." The princess thought if she went to rescue the prince then she too would be taken prisoner. But then she had an idea. She cut off her beautiful, long hair and dressed in boy's clothes. Then she took her lute and set off to rescue her husband.

The brave princess travelled through many lands dressed as a boy and playing her lute, before she reached the palace where the prince was in prison. She went into the palace and played her lute and sang as beautifully as she could. The mean king listened, and thought it was the lovliest sound he had ever heard. He told her, "Stay

here and play for a few days.
When you leave I will give you
whatever you ask for."

So the princess played her
lute in the palace for three
days, then she asked the king
for one of his prisoners. "It will
be nice to have a friend to
travel with," she said. So the
king allowed the princess to
choose a prisoner, and she
chose her husband, although she

pretended not to know him.

The couple set off on the long journey home. But the princess was still dressed as a boy and the prince didn't realize he was travelling with his wife. Although he asked many questions, he never found out who she was. All the time the secret princess was leading him back home.

When they were almost at

the palace, the princess slipped away. She took a short cut and arrived before the prince. She changed into a beautiful dress and waited outside the palace.

The Secret Princess

As the prince arrived, a crowd was cheering, "Our prince is home!" But the prince was angry with his wife because he thought she hadn't helped him.

BRAVE AND BOLD

So as the prince was talking
to his people, the princess
slipped away again and changed
back into boy's clothing. Then
she came and stood before her
husband and started playing the
lute and singing sweetly.

The prince realized that his
wife was really disguised as the
lute player all along, and that
she had rescued him. He was
sorry that he had doubted her.

The Secret Princess

The prince put on a great feast
for his wife, and everyone
celebrated for a week.

The Twelve Brothers

Once there was a king and queen who had twelve sons. One day the king said to the queen, "If our thirteenth child is a girl, we must imprison our sons and give all our land and

The Twelve Brothers

possessions to our daughter."
This made the queen very
sad, so she came up with a plan
for her sons. "You must run
away into the woods and
find somewhere to hide
where no one can
find you." So the
brothers ran away
and found a magic
house in the woods
where they lived for

the next ten years.

Meanwhile the King and queen had a baby girl. She grew up to be good and Kind and always wore a gold star on her head. One day, when she was sixteen years old, the princess

The Twelve Brothers

noticed twelve white shirts drying on the washing line. She asked her mother who the shirts belonged to. The queen replied, "My dear, those shirts belong to your twelve brothers." The queen

told the princess how her
brothers had been forced to run
away when she was a baby, and
the queen began to cry.

"Please don't cry mother,"
said the princess. "I will go and
find my brothers." She took the
twelve shirts and bravely set off
into the woods.

The princess walked all day,
and by night came to the house
in the woods where her brothers

lived. They asked her who she was and why she was there. When the princess told them her story, the princes said that they were her long-lost brothers. So they all lived happily in the house in the woods, until one day something happened.

There was a garden around the house where twelve tall, white flowers grew. The princess wanted to give each brother a flower, so she picked them from the garden. But as soon as she did this, the brothers were changed into ravens. They flew away over the woods, leaving their sister alone.

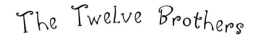

Suddenly, the princess saw an old woman standing nearby so she asked, "How can I break the spell and free my brothers?"

The old woman said, "You must not speak or make any sound for seven years." So the poor princess began her lonely life of silence.

One day, a few years later, a

king came riding past the house and noticed the beautiful princess with a gold star on her head as she walked in the garden. He asked her to be his wife. But as the princess couldn't talk, she simply nodded, and went with the king to his palace where they were married.

The king's mother didn't like the beautiful princess. She said nasty things about her to the king. At first the King didn't believe his mother. But because the princess couldn't speak and tell her husband the truth, he began to believe what his mother said. At last, he decided to send the princess to prison.

Just as guards arrived to take the princess, the seven years came to an end – the spell was broken! Suddenly, twelve ravens flew down from

the sky. The ravens turned back
into the princess's brothers as
they landed, and they quickly

set their sister free. At last the princess could speak and she told the king her story. The king was so happy when he heard that all the things his mother had said were not true. His mother was sent away, and everyone lived happily ever after.

The Girl and the Lion

There was once a poor girl who looked after cows. One morning she was taking her cows through a field when she heard a loud growl. There in the grass she saw a lion sitting

The Girl and the Lion

holding up its paw. The girl could see a big thorn, which looked very painful. She bravely removed the thorn and bandaged the lion's paw.

BRAVE AND BOLD

When the girl went back to her cows they were gone. She looked everywhere but couldn't find them. Her master was cross with her for letting them escape. In their place he gave her his donkeys to look after.

Every day the girl took the donkeys to graze in the woods. Then one morning, she heard a growl. She saw the same lion lying on the ground, this time

with a big cut across his face.
The girl was not at all afraid,
and she rushed over to the lion
to wash his cut.

When the girl went back to
her donkeys they too had
disappeared. She looked for
them everywhere but couldn't
find them. Her master was even
more cross than the last time.
This time he gave her his pigs
to look after.

BRAVE AND BOLD

The next day she took the pigs out to feed, and the day after that. On the following day the girl heard a growl for a third time. She found her old friend the lion, with a cut paw, lying under a tree. The girl washed and bandaged the paw to make it better.

Then she went back to her pigs, but just like the cows and the donkeys, the pigs

109

had gone. She climbed a tree to get a better view of the land. Soon night fell, and as she sat in the branches the girl saw something strange. A young man pulled aside a rock from a cave and crept behind it. The girl stayed in the tree all night. In the morning, the lion came out from behind the rock.

The Girl and the Lion

She waited until nightfall, then the man appeared again. The girl asked him who he was. The man told her that he was really a prince, and that a giant had put a spell on him. So he was a lion by day and a prince at night. The girl asked how she could break the spell.

BRAVE AND BOLD

"You need to get a lock of hair from a princess and spin it into a coat for the giant."

So the girl went to work in the palace, where she made sure that her hair always looked beautiful. The princess noticed this, and asked the girl to do her hair too. Every day the girl combed the princess's hair so that it shone like the sun. One day the girl dared to ask the

princess for a lock of her hair. "You may have a lock of my hair if you find me a prince to marry," said the princess. So the girl cut off a lock of the princess's hair and spun it into a glittering coat. Then she climbed a mountain to take the coat to the giant.

She bravely presented the coat to the giant, who was pleased with the gift.

"In return, you may have one wish," the giant said. The girl asked for the spell to be removed from the prince so he was no longer a lion.

The Girl and the Lion

The giant said, "To break the spell, you must kill the lion and cut him into pieces. Then the pieces must be burnt and thrown into a lake."

The girl returned to the prince and told him what the giant had said. She was scared it was a trick and didn't want to kill the lion.

"Be brave and do it," the prince told her. So the girl did

everything the giant had said.

   Then out of the lake walked
the prince, as handsome as
could be! He thanked the girl
for saving him and asked her to
marry him. But she wept, and

The Girl and the Lion

told him of her promise to the princess. So they went to the palace to see the princess. When the princess saw the prince she was so happy, as he was her long-lost brother.

The prince and the girl were married, and they lived happily ever after.

The Princess and the Hare

There was once a queen who wanted a child. One day the queen said to the sun, "Please sun, send me a little girl. When she is twelve years old, I will give her back to you."

The Princess and the Hare

Soon after this, the Sun sent the queen a little girl, whom she called Letiko. The queen loved her little princess dearly. When Letiko was twelve, the sun said to her one day, "Tell your mother to remember what she said to me." Letiko went home and told the queen this.

The queen was scared that the sun would come to take her daughter away. She shut all the

BRAVE AND BOLD

doors and windows of the palace and hid Letiko. But she forgot to close up the keyhole. The sun shone through the keyhole and took Letiko away. She went to live with the sun to do his work.

Letiko was unhappy, as she missed her mother. One day the sun heard Letiko crying. This made him sad, so he asked two hares to take Letiko home.

The hares and Letiko set off. But before long, the hares grew hungry, and asked Letiko to hide in a tree while they ate.

"Dear Letiko, wait in this tree until we've finished eating some grass." So Letiko climbed the tree and the hares went

off to find some grass.

A witch had seen Letiko climb the tree. She said, "Letiko, Letiko, come down from the tree and look at my beautiful shoes."

But Princess Letiko replied, "My shoes are more beautiful than your shoes. Go away!"

So then the witch said, "Letiko, Letiko, come down from the tree and look at my fine apron."

But brave Letiko replied, "My apron is finer than your apron. Go away!"

The witch went away, but returned with an axe and said, "If you will not come down, I will cut down the tree and eat you!"

Letiko cried, "Chop down the tree and eat me, then!" So the witch chopped at the tree, but she couldn't cut it down.

When the witch had gone,

Letiko cried, "Little
hares! Come back!"
The hares heard
Letiko and ran back as
fast as they could. Letiko
came down from the tree and
told them about the witch. They
hurried on to the palace. But the
witch hadn't gone far, and was
soon chasing after them.

When Letiko was nearly
at the palace, the queen's

dog recognized her. It rushed out and cried, "Bow wow! Letiko is home!"

Then the queen's cat also saw Letiko and cried, "Meow, Meow! Letiko is home!"

But the queen didn't believe them and said, "Be quiet!"

Letiko and the hares

ran into the the palace, but the
witch was close behind them.
She grabbed the tail of one
hare before it got inside, and
pulled the tail off before the
door was slammed in her face.

The queen saw the little hare
without a tail and said, "Dear
hare, because you have brought
my Letiko home, I will give you a
silver tail in place of the tail
you've lost." So she did, and the

hare with the silver tail and the other hare, his best friend, lived happily ever after with Princess Letiko.

The Princess and the Jelly Castle

Once upon a time there was a shy princess called Daisy who was scared of most things. So you can imagine how worried Princess Daisy was when the king and queen told her they were giving her a birthday party, and young princesses and princes from neighbouring lands were invited.

On the day of her party Princess Daisy hid upstairs in her bedroom. She was too scared to meet all of her guests. The queen held Daisy's hand and together they walked downstairs. Daisy looked beautiful in her sparkly purple dress and she wore a little purple and gold crown. But all the way to the garden, Daisy looked down at the ground, as she was too frightened to look up. "You're doing great," whispered her mother.

Fairy lights were hung around the garden and all the royal children wore their best clothes. By the pond was the biggest jelly castle you've ever seen!

The Princess and the Jelly Castle

131

BRAVE AND BOLD

"Come and play Pin the Tail on the Dragon," said Princess Candy to Daisy. So Daisy shyly followed. Candy covered Daisy's eyes with a scarf, then spun her around. Daisy wasn't very good at the game and pinned the tail on the wrong end of the dragon. She thought the other children must be laughing at her and her face turned bright red.

Next Daisy tried the Golden

Egg and Spoon Race. But she dropped the egg at the start and quickly ran and hid behind the king. "I'm not very good at any of the games," she said.

"It doesn't matter. Just try your best," said the king.

Then Prince Theo asked Daisy to have a race with him. But Daisy's knees were shaking and she was too scared to move. Just at that moment she looked across the garden and saw Prince Butterfingers carrying a plate of sausages. He wasn't looking where he was going and he was walking towards the deep pond – and he couldn't swim!

Without thinking, Daisy ran as fast as she could across the garden and pushed Prince Butterfingers out of the way, just in time! Everyone at the

The Princess and the Jelly Castle

party stopped talking and
looked at Daisy and
Prince Butterfingers.
They had both
fallen in the jelly
castle and were
covered from
head to toe in
sticky pink jelly!
Then Daisy
looked at Prince
Butterfingers,

and they both burst out
laughing.

Prince Theo ran
up to Daisy and
said, "You won the
race!" and he
gave Daisy a
rosette. Brave
Princess Daisy
had saved Prince
Butterfingers and
she had also

won a race. She had quite forgotten her shyness. This was the best birthday party ever!

The Iron Oven

A long time ago a witch put a wicked spell on a prince and shut him in a large iron oven in the woods.

One day a princess, who was lost in the woods, came across

The Iron Oven

the oven. She was shocked to hear a voice coming from inside it. The voice said, "I am a prince and can help you find your way home."

In return for helping the princess get home, the prince asked her to return with a knife to help free him from the oven. The prince also said that he would marry the princess if she helped him.

So the princess did everything the prince asked. Then she made a hole in the oven with the knife and worked hard until the hole was big enough for the prince to climb out of. He was very handsome and the princess fell in love with him at once. He asked her to go with him to his castle and get

married. But the princess
wanted to tell her father the
happy news.

"Very well," said the prince,

"but be careful, as you must not speak more than three words, if you do, the spell I am under cannot be broken."

The princess said she wouldn't, and ran back to her father. But as soon as she got home, she was so excited that she spoke more than three words. Immediately a wind blew any memory of the princess from the prince's head, and sent

The Iron Oven

him back to his castle. When the princess ran back into the woods she couldn't find the prince anywhere.

After nine days of looking for the prince, the princess found a little house in the woods, which was home to a family of toads. The princess explained what had happened, and the toads told her where she could find the prince's palace. They gave her a magic nut and told her to open it whenever she needed help. Then they wished her good luck.

The brave princess travelled over a glass mountain, a field with plants as sharp as swords and a huge lake. At last she reached the prince's castle. But after walking for so long the princess's clothes were dirty and torn, and she didn't look like a princess at all. How could she go

The Iron Oven

to the castle to see her prince
looking like that?
Suddenly,
the princess
remembered

the magic nut that the kind
toads had given to her.
She used a stone to prise open
the nut. Inside was the most
beautiful dress she had ever
seen – it was made of glittering
gold and shone like the sun.

The princess put on the
dress and knocked at the castle
gates. As soon as the prince
saw her he remembered who
she was, and threw his arms

The Iron Oven

around her. The spell was broken! They were married that day, and lived happily ever after.

The Crow

Once upon a time there were three princesses. They were all beautiful but the youngest was the

The Crow

kindest. There was an old castle near the princesses' palace, which had a lovely flower garden. The youngest princess loved to go walking there.

One day, the princess was in the garden and a crow hopped in front of her. The poor crow was bleeding and its feathers were

149

torn. This made the princess sad. But the crow said to her, "I am really a prince who has been changed into a crow by a witch."

The crow asked the princess to leave her home and live with him in the old castle to break the spell. At once the kind princess agreed. She said goodbye to her family and went to live in the old castle. She was given a room with a golden bed,

The Crow

and the crow said to her, "You must not make a sound at night, no matter what you see."

When night came the princess was afraid, and she couldn't sleep. Then at midnight, her door was flung open and a huge green dragon came in. It breathed hot fire near the princess's bed. But she lay still and didn't make a sound.

The dragon disappeared and

next a big brown bear stomped
into the room. The bear roared,

The Crow

showing its sharp teeth. Still the princess was quiet. Next a huge monster came in and leapt towards the princess, but she remained still and quiet. Then the monster, too,

153

disappeared. For many nights, strange creatures came into the princess's room but the princess was brave and didn't make a sound. The crow thanked the princess for being so brave and told her he was getting better.

One day the crow said, "Soon I shall be free from this wicked spell. But now I need you to work as a maid for a while." So the princess did as she was

The Crow

asked. The people she worked for were unkind and made the princess work hard. But still she carried on.

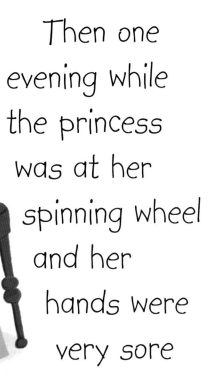

Then one evening while the princess was at her spinning wheel and her hands were very sore

155

from spinning all day, a young man knelt beside her and kissed her hands.

"I am the prince who was once the crow you helped," he said. "Your kindness has finally freed me from the wicked spell."

The prince took the princess back to the crumbling castle – but it was not an old castle anymore. It had been repaired and painted, and was now a

The Crow

beautiful, shining palace. The prince and princess were married and lived there happily for the rest of their days.

CLEVER PRINCESSES

A Troublesome Dragon

Once upon a time in a faraway land a King asked his advisors, "Who can get rid of the dragon that's eating our food and scaring my people?"

The King's daughter, Princess

A Troublesome Dragon

Iris, said, "I'll get rid of the dragon, father."

But the King replied, "Don't you worry about the dragon my dear. My brave knights will help to solve this problem."

The first knight to step forward to help was called Sir Tickle. He got his name from a long blue feather that hung from his helmet and tickled his face. Everyone knows that dragons hate water, so Sir Tickle set off with a long hose to the dragon's cave, which was on a nearby hill. But the dragon saw Sir Tickle coming. He pressed a button on his magic belt and a cape covered him up.

Sir Tickle shouted to a servant, "Turn on the tap!" and water poured over the dragon. But the

162

163

cape kept him dry. Sir Tickle went back to the King and told him that the dragon was too clever for him.

The next Knight to try and get rid of the dragon was Sir Bright. He liked to wear bright clothes – so he was the perfect Knight to face the dragon, as dragons hate bright colours, especially red. Sir Bright dressed from head to toe in

red, and even put a red coat
on his horse.

When the clever dragon saw
Sir Bright trotting boldly
towards him on his horse, again
he pressed a button on his
magic belt. This time a pair of
special glasses popped over his
eyes. Even when Sir Bright and
his horse stood right in front of
the dragon wearing their bright
red clothes, he wasn't bothered

at all. He found it very funny and
laughed really hard! Sir Bright
went back to the king and said
the dragon was too wise.

A Troublesome Dragon

Secretly, Princess Iris had followed each knight to the dragon's cave and she noticed that the dragon always wore a belt. The clever princess guessed that the belt was magic, and that this helped the dragon to stop the knights.

One night, Princess Iris crept out of the palace to the dragon's cave. The dragon was snoring loudly, and the princess

carefully tiptoed around him.
The dragon's magic belt was
lying on the floor. Princess Iris
dragged the belt out of the cave
– it was too heavy for her to
carry. She pulled it into a field
and buried it.

Then Princess Iris went back
to the palace, and got the hose
and put on a red cape. Day was
breaking and the dragon was
waking up. He fumbled around

A Troublesome Dragon

his cave for his magic belt but it wasn't there. Someone had stolen it! The dragon was very angry. He stormed out of his cave to look for the thief, just as Princess Iris arrived. Her bright red cape hurt the dragon's eyes.

Suddenly the princess sprayed water all over the dragon. He was drenched! Not only did the dragon hate bright colours, he hated being wet, too.

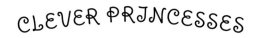

"I'm not staying here anymore!" he growled as he flapped his wings and flew off in a huff.

A Troublesome Dragon

And from that day on, if the king needed any help he always asked clever Princess Iris first.

The Dreadful Giant

One day, a princess was playing catch with her ball in the garden. She threw the ball much higher than ever before, and it never came down.

"Aargh!" a loud voice roared

The Dreadful Giant

from high up in the sky.
   Suddenly, a palace guard
appeared and whisked the
princess away to a castle on
a mountain. He took
her to a tower
that was filled
with white cats.

"Your ball hit a giant in the eye, and that was the giant you heard shouting," said the guard. He told the princess that giants hate white cats, so to keep her safe, she would now live at the Castle of the White Cats.

The princess was so happy playing with the cats that she soon forgot about the giant. But the giant hadn't forgotten about her. "Cats love mice better than princesses," the giant said. So he filled a large sack with hundreds of fat mice and went to the castle.

The princess could see a long way from her tower, and she spotted the giant heading towards the castle with a large sack. The clever princess guessed what the giant was carrying. "I will give you hundreds more mice and much fatter mice than the giant," she told the cats.

When the giant let the mice out of the sack they ran all over the castle, but the cats didn't chase after them. They could hear the mice and smell the mice, but not one cat moved! So the giant returned home in a very bad mood.

"Cats love sparrows more than princesses," said the giant.

The Dreadful Giant

So this time he filled a big cage with lots of fat sparrows. But once again the princess saw the giant coming to the castle from her tower, and she guessed what he was planning.

177

"I will give you hundreds more sparrows, and much fatter ones than the giant," the princess said to the cats. So again when the giant released the sparrows over the castle, not one cat moved. And the giant went home again huffing and puffing with anger.

Next the giant got some magic powder from a wise frog. When he poured water onto the powder it turned blue. So the giant set off to the castle with a large jug of blue water. But again the clever princess was one step ahead of him.

When the giant reached the castle, he shut his eyes (because giants don't like looking at white cats) and poured the blue water over the cats. He also slopped blue water all over himself. So the white cats, and the giant, turned bright blue. But at least the giant could open his eyes. He stomped up to the highest room in the castle and burst in. But the clever princess was nowhere to be seen.

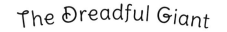

The Dreadful Giant

A fairy had
flown over the palace
as the giant approached with
the blue water. The princess
asked for her help, so the fairy
changed the princess into a tiny
flea, which meant the giant
couldn't see her.

The blue giant stormed out

of the castle grunting and muttering. He was so angry that he didn't look where he was going, and he walked right off the edge of the mountain – and that was the end of the dreadful giant.

Meanwhile, the fairy changed the flea back into the princess, and all the cats were given a bubble bath to get the blue colour out of their fur. In no

time they were pure white again, and they lived happily ever after in the castle with the princess.

183

The Clever Tailor

Once upon a time there was a very proud, but clever princess. If a man asked to marry her she would give him a riddle. And when he couldn't guess the riddle he would be sent away. The princess said, "I will only marry the man who can guess my riddle."

One day three tailors went to the palace and begged the princess to give them a riddle. The princess said, "I have two

different colours of hair on my
head. What colours are they?"
The first tailor guessed black
and white, while the second
tailor guessed red and brown.
These answers were both wrong.
The third tailor who was the
youngest said, "The princess has
gold and silver hair." The
princess turned pale as the
tailor had got her question right.
She said, "Don't think you

have won yet! You have still have one more thing to do." And the princess told the youngest tailor that he had to sleep in a stable with a bear for the night. She knew that the bear had killed everyone who had entered the stable. "If you are still alive in the morning, I will marry you," said the princess.

So the youngest tailor was taken to the stable. The bear

had very sharp claws and was very fierce. It growled at the tailor. But the tailor said, "Be gentle," to the bear, and he started eating some nuts.

The bear wanted to eat nuts too, so he asked the tailor for some. But the tailor gave the bear pebbles instead of nuts. The bear found it hard to eat pebbles, and the tailor made fun of him. "What? You cannot

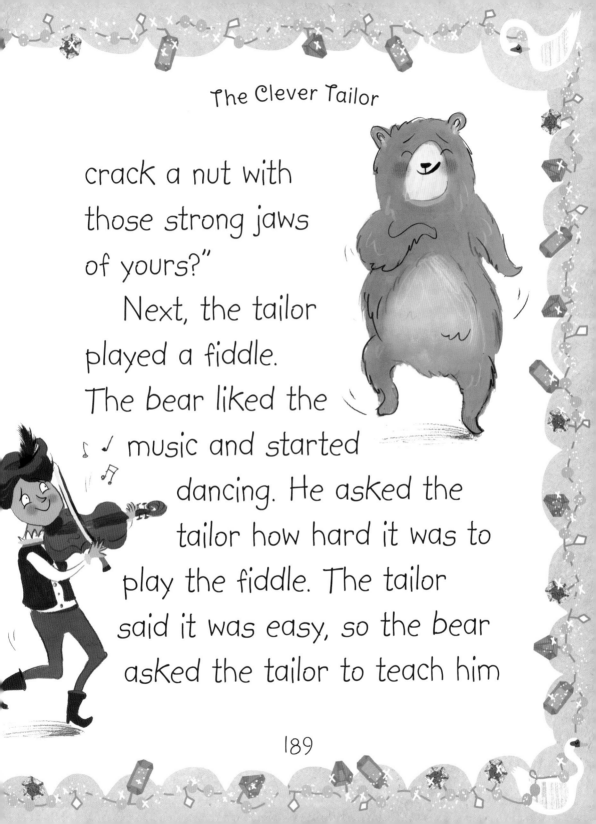

The Clever Tailor

crack a nut with those strong jaws of yours?"

Next, the tailor played a fiddle. The bear liked the music and started dancing. He asked the tailor how hard it was to play the fiddle. The tailor said it was easy, so the bear asked the tailor to teach him to play. The tailor replied, "Your claws are very long. I must cut them first."

So the bear let the tailor tie his paws together so that he could cut his claws. But instead the tailor tied the bear's paws so that he couldn't move! Then the tailor went to sleep.

The next morning the princess went to the stable thinking that the bear would

The Clever Tailor

have killed the tailor. But the tailor stood in front of the stable door, smiling. After this, the princess knew she had met a man who was as clever as her. She married the tailor and they both lived happily ever after.

The Ruby Prince

There once was a king who was given a beautiful red, ruby stone. The stone was wrapped in cotton wool and locked in a chest. After twelve years the king wanted to see his ruby, so the chest was brought before him and unlocked. To everyone's surprise a young man jumped out. "Who are you?" asked the king. "And where is my ruby?"

The young man replied, "I am the Ruby Prince." When the king's daughter and the Ruby Prince met, they fell in love. They were married and given half of the king's land.

The princess loved her handsome husband but was sad because she didn't know anything about him. Every day she asked her husband where he was from, but every day he said, "I cannot tell you that."

Then one day, the Ruby Prince and the princess were

The Ruby Prince

walking by a lake. The princess begged her husband to tell her where he was from. Suddenly there appeared a giant snake wearing a golden crown, and in a puff the Ruby Prince was gone.

The princess went home with a heavy heart.

She offered a reward to anyone who could tell her where her Ruby Prince had gone. Weeks went by with no news. Then one day, a dancing-girl told the princess what had happened when she was collecting wood and had fallen asleep by a tree.

"I woke up and saw some young men coming out of a hole in the tree. They wore jewels and danced before a snake king.

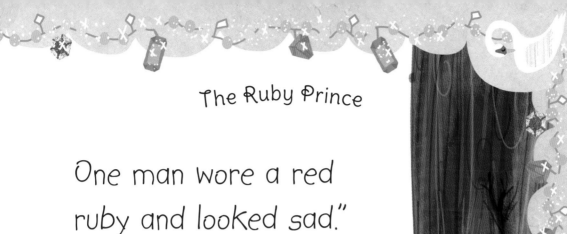

One man wore a red
ruby and looked sad."
     The next night the
princess went with the
dancing-girl to the tree.
Just as the girl had said,
some men came
out of the tree,
and one man was
wearing a ruby. The princess
recognized her husband, the
Ruby Prince, but she was sad to

see he was so unhappy. Every night after that, the princess went to the tree to watch her husband, and every night she was sad that she couldn't speak to him.

But the clever princess came up with a plan. She said, "The snake king loves dancing. What if I was able to dance beautifully for him? He may give me anything I ask for!" So the princess asked the dancing-girl to teach her how to dance. She was very graceful, and was soon better than the dancing-girl herself.

One night, the princess dressed in a beautiful gown and sparkling jewels so that she shone like a star. She hid behind the tree and waited for the men to come out. When they appeared, the Ruby Prince

looked sadder than ever. The princess stepped out from behind the tree and danced before the snake king.

The snake king cried out, "O dancer that no one knows, ask for anything and it will be yours." The

The Ruby Prince

princess asked for the Ruby Prince. The snake king knew he had been tricked. But he said, "Take him and go!"

So the princess and the Ruby Prince ran home, where they lived happily every after. And the princess never asked the Ruby Prince where he came from again.

The Wise Girl

There was once a girl who was wiser than the King. Her father was so proud of her that he told everyone how clever she was. One day he said, "My daughter is so clever that she could answer any question that the King asked."

The King heard about this, and the next day he gave the man thirty eggs for his daughter to hatch. The King said, "Only a clever person could make these eggs hatch." So the man gave the eggs to his daughter, but the girl realized that the eggs had been boiled and would not hatch. But her father was afraid to take them back to the king.

The girl gave her father a bag of boiled beans. She told him to pretend to plant the beans by the road when the king passed by. The king didn't recognize the man. He stopped and said, "My poor man, how can you think boiled beans will grow?"

The Wise Girl

205

The man replied as his daughter had instructed him: "Whatever the King asks can be done. If boiled eggs can hatch into chickens, then why can't boiled beans grow?" The King remembered giving the eggs to the man the day before. He said, "Your daughter is clever."

Next the King gave the man some flax for his daughter to turn into the sails of a big ship.

The Wise Girl

The man went home and gave
the flax to his daughter. He was
worried, but his daughter told
him to go to bed.

The next day the girl gave
her father a small piece of
wood. She said, "Tell the King
when he has made a big wooden
ship from this small piece of
wood, I will turn the flax into
some sails for it."

Her father did this and the

King was surprised at the clever
girl's answer. He sent for the girl
to come to the palace.

The Wise Girl

She stood in front of the King in her plain dress and old shoes. The King was happy with her answers and knew he wanted her to be his queen. But the girl said, "I am poor and we may not be happy. You may want to send me back to my father. Promise me that if this happens I can take home what is most dear to me." The King agreed, and they were married.

After she became queen the girl wore beautiful dresses and jewels. But the King grew jealous and thought she cared more about her dresses than him. He told her to go back to her father.

But the girl wanted to take with

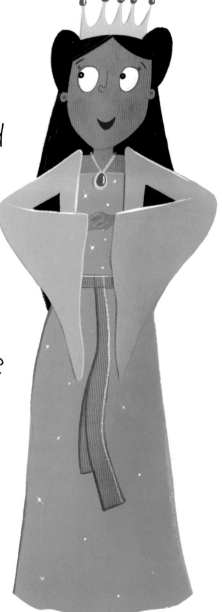

210

her the thing she held most dear. She gave the king a drink with some sleeping powder in it. He fell asleep immediately, and the girl arranged for servants to take him to her old home.

When the king awoke, he was surprised to be in her father's house. "What does this mean?" he asked.

"You promised that if I was ever sent back to my father I

could take with me the thing
that was most dear to me. Well,
I've taken you because you are

the most dear to me!"

Of course after that, the King wasn't jealous or angry any more. They went back to the palace and lived together in great happiness.

The Giant Who Counted Carrots

Once upon a time there was a giant who lived beneath the mountains. One morning he decided to take a walk above the mountains. As he did, he saw a beautiful princess sitting beside a rock pool. The giant fell in love with the princess, and decided to try to win her heart. He changed the rocks into glittering jewels and put a sparkling fountain in the middle of the pool.

The princess wanted more than anything to paddle in the beautiful rock pool. But as soon as she dipped her bare feet in the water, she was dragged

under. Down, down, down she sank...and then she was gone!

The princess had been dragged beneath the mountains to the giant's magical palace. But the giant didn't want to hurt the princess. He showed her all round his palace and gardens, where he grew rows and rows of tasty vegetables.

So the princess stayed with the giant. But the splendid palace and gardens were not enough to put a smile on the princess's face. This was because she was missing her friends and family, but she didn't tell the giant. The giant saw that the princess was

unhappy, and then he
remembered his magic wand.
Whatever it touched would turn
into anything he
wished for. So
the giant gave the
wand to the princess.
She wished for her
little dog Benny,
and her friends.
For a while the princess was
happy again, but the magic

The Giant Who Counted Carrots

didn't last for long and her pet
and friends soon disappeared.

Meanwhile a young prince,
who had won the heart of the
princess back home, wandered
over the mountains looking for
his love, but the clever princess
had thought up a plan to
escape. She pretended to the
giant that she was in love with
him, and one day she said, "How
can I be sure you love me?"

The giant replied, "Give me a test, my love." So the princess told the giant to go and count all of the carrots in his field. At once, the giant rushed off to do as the princess asked and show his love for her.

But as soon as he had gone, the princess used the magic wand to turn a potato into a horse. She leapt on the horse's back and galloped out from

The Giant Who Counted Carrots

under the mountains straight into the arms of her prince. And she left the giant still counting carrots in the garden!

The Bamboo Cutter and the Moon Child

A long time ago there lived an old woodcutter and his wife. They were sad because they never had any children.

One morning the woodcutter was chopping bamboo when a

The Bamboo Cutter and the Moon Child

bright light shone out of one of the stems. Inside, the woodcutter found a beautiful, tiny girl. He said, "You are meant to be my child." And he took the girl home, to care for with his wife.

They called the young girl

Princess Moonlight. Everyone said she was beautiful and when she grew up many men wanted to marry her.

One day, five knights came to the house to see Princess Moonlight. They had travelled a long way and waited for days outside the house. Her father felt sorry for the knights and asked his daughter to see them. But clever Princess Moonlight said that she knew nothing about them and that she wanted to give the knights a test before meeting them.

So the princess asked each knight to find something. The first knight had to find a special stone bowl from India. But he didn't want to travel all the way to India, so he found another stone bowl, wrapped it in gold cloth and sent it to the princess.

But when the princess unwrapped the bowl, it didn't shine. The clever princess knew it was not the special bowl she had asked for.

The second knight had to get a branch from a gold and silver tree that grew up a mountain, far away across the sea. The knight set off but his journey across the sea was hard and he soon gave up. So he asked some jewellers to make him a gold and silver branch. The princess looked at the branch and knew it was not the one she had asked for.

The princess told the third knight to go to China to find the fire rat and send its skin to her. But the knight didn't go to

China. Instead he paid a friend who lived in China to send him the skin of a fire rat. The friend took the money but sent a different animal's skin instead. The princess knew that the skin of the real fire rat would not burn so she threw the skin into the fire. The skin burnt at once and the princess knew the knight had tried to trick her.

The fourth knight had to find a dragon with a magic stone. The knight was lazy, so he told his servants to look for the dragon. But after a year his servants couldn't find it, so the knight gave up his search.

The princess told the fifth

Knight to find a bird with a special shell in its tummy. The fifth knight was lazy like all the others, and he soon gave up his search, too. All the knights, and many after that, were sent home for trying to trick the clever princess.

Then one day, the woodcutter found his daughter crying and asked her what was wrong. She said, "I have come from the moon and soon I have to go back to the moon." The princess was sad that she had to leave the woodcutter and his wife.

The woodcutter didn't want his daughter to go, either. So he told everyone in the house to watch over the princess at night and make sure that no one took her away. Even the king heard and sent his soldiers to guard Princess Moonlight.

But one night a cloud came
down from the moon. A grand
King was in the cloud and said

232

he had come to take Princess Moonlight home. The princess knew it was time to go back, so she stepped into the cloud. She was sad to leave the woodcutter and his wife, and said to them, "Thank you for taking good care of me. Think of me when you look up at the moon."

The Twelve Dancing Princesses

There once was a King who had twelve beautiful daughters. They slept in twelve beds all in one big room and when they went to bed each night their bedroom door was

locked. But every morning their shoes were worn out, as if they had been dancing all night long. The King was at his wits end and said, "Whoever can find out where the princesses go at night can choose a princess to marry."

CLEVER PRINCESSES

Many princes had a go at guessing the clever princesses' secret. One night, a prince was even given a room next door to the princesses' bedroom. He left his door open so that he could see if they left their room. He should have kept watch all night, but soon fell fast asleep. In the morning he discovered that the princesses had been dancing all night again, and that their shoes were quite worn out.

One day a soldier was passing through the town when he met an old woman. He told her that he wanted to find out the princesses' secret.

"Then you must not drink the milk that the eldest princess will give you," said the old woman. "When she leaves, you must just pretend to be asleep."

Then the old woman gave the

soldier a cloak and told him that
when he put it on he
would be invisible.

The soldier
arrived at the
palace and was
shown to the
room next to
the princesses'
bedroom. Just
as he was
settling down,

the eldest princess brought him
a glass of milk. When she
wasn't looking the soldier tipped
the milk away and then
pretended to fall asleep. The
princess laughed and went back
to her sisters. The soldier heard
the princesses giggling in their
bedroom as they excitedly got
dressed to go dancing.

When the princesses were
ready they checked the soldier

CLEVER PRINCESSES

was asleep. He was snoring, so they went back into their room and the eldest princess clapped her hands. A trapdoor opened, and the princesses hurried down some steps.

The soldier saw all of this as he had only pretended to be asleep. He jumped up, put on the magic cloak and quickly followed the princesses down the steps. The youngest princess thought she heard someone behind her. But the cloak made the soldier invisible so she couldn't see him.

The steps led to a lake upon which beautiful swans were

CLEVER PRINCESSES

swimming, and where twelve boats with twelve princes were waiting for the princesses. The solider hopped into the boat with the eldest princess.

Twelve Dancing Princesses

They reached the other side
of the lake where a glittering
castle stood. The invisible soldier
followed the princesses and the
princes inside, where they
danced all night until their shoes
were worn out. Then the soldier
followed as the princes rowed
the princesses back across the
lake and said goodbye.

The soldier ran up the steps
ahead of the princesses and lay

down in his room and snored.
When the princesses returned
they heard him snoring and
said, "We are safe."

The next morning the King
asked the soldier where his
daughters went to dance at
night. The soldier said, "They
dance with twelve princes in a
castle underground." And he told
the King what he had seen.

The princesses Knew their

secret was out and told their father it was true. The King asked the soldier which princess he would like to marry.

"I would like to marry the eldest princess, if she will marry me." The princess was happy to marry a man as clever as her, and they lived happily ever after.

MAGIC AND ENCHANTMENT

The Little Mermaid

In a castle deep under the sea lived a sea king and his six daughters, who were sea princesses, or mermaids. The youngest mermaid was the most beautiful, with eyes as blue as the sea. Like her sisters she had no legs or feet and her body ended in a shimmering, green fishtail.

Outside the castle was a beautiful garden of bright, colourful sea flowers. Each of the mermaid princesses had a little plot of ground in the garden that was theirs to tend. The youngest mermaid loved nothing more than looking after

her flowers as she gazed at a
stone statue of a boy that had
fallen to the
bottom of
the sea
long ago.

She also loved listening to her grandmother's stories of the world above the sea.

"When you are fifteen," said her grandmother, "you can go above the sea and sit on the rocks in the moonlight." The youngest princess longed to see the world above the sea. "I wish I was fifteen years old right now," she said. "I know I will love the world above, and all the people who live in it."

At last the youngest princess turned fifteen. She waved goodbye to her sisters and rose as lightly as a bubble to the top of the sea. A large ship sat on the water. The little mermaid swam as close to the ship as she dared, and when the waves lifted her she could see the people onboard.

The Little Mermaid

She saw a young prince with dark eyes. It was his sixteenth birthday and there was dancing and fireworks. The fireworks frightened the little mermaid and she dived back under the sea. But then she came up again as she couldn't keep her eyes off the beautiful prince.

After a while the ship set sail. But suddenly a storm came from nowhere. The waves were

so high, and the ship was tossed up and down. Suddenly, the prince was thrown into the sea. The little mermaid swam to help him and held his head

The Little Mermaid

above the water. She swam with
the prince to land and laid him
on the beach. The prince
started to wake up, but the little
mermaid had to return to her
father's castle under the sea.
The prince didn't know that she
had saved him.

From then on, the little
mermaid would spend many
nights in the water near the
prince's palace to watch him.

She wished more than anything
that she could live in his world.

So one day she went to the
sea witch who lived in deep,
dark water. The little mermaid
had never been to that part of
the sea before. She was so
scared that she almost changed
her mind. But then she thought
of how much she wanted to be
with the prince above the sea.

"I know what you want," said

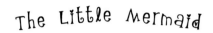

The Little Mermaid

the sea witch, and she gave the
little mermaid a special drink.
She told her to swim to land,

and then take the drink. "Your tail will disappear and you will grow legs," said the sea witch. "But once you are a person you can never be a mermaid again. And if the prince marries another, you will die!"

The little mermaid also had to give the sea witch her voice in return for the special drink, so she could never speak again. At last she swam up to the prince's

palace and took the drink. Her
tail disappeared and she grew
legs. When the prince found her
on the beach, he took her back
to his palace and made sure
she was well cared for and
dressed in fine clothes.

The little mermaid and the
prince spent all their time
together, and the prince said
she would always be by his side.
As time passed the little

mermaid loved the prince more and more, and he loved her. But he didn't think of her as a wife.

Then one day the prince sailed away to meet a princess who his parents wanted him to marry. The little mermaid went too. When the prince saw the princess, he fell in love with her, and they were married.

When everyone was having fun at the wedding, the little

mermaid blew the prince a kiss
and slipped away into the sea.
But she did not die. Instead she
was lifted up by spirits, and
flew around the world
with them doing
good deeds.

Earl Mar's Daughter

It was a fine summer's day as Earl Mar's daughter was walking in the castle gardens. She looked up and saw a dove sitting in an oak tree. She said, "My dear little dove, fly down to me. I will take you home and keep you as my pet." As she spoke, the dove flew onto her shoulder, so she took it home with her.

But as night came Earl Mar's daughter was surprised to find a handsome young man sitting by her bed. "I am that dove you brought home," he said, and he told her that he was really a prince called Florentine, and his mother had put a spell on him.

"She changed me into a dove by day. But at night her spell loses its power and I am a man again," he said.

The prince said he would love Earl Mar's daughter forever and never leave her side if she married him. So the prince and Earl Mar's daughter were married in secret. They lived happily in the castle and no one

Earl Mar's Daughter

knew that every night the little white dove changed into Prince Florentine, and that every year a little son was born to Earl Mar's daughter. Prince Florentine flew over the sea with their baby son

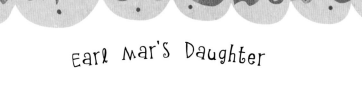

on his back, and left the baby with his mother.

After seven years Earl Mar said it was time

his daughter got married. He
didn't know that she was
already secretly married to
Prince Florentine. His daughter
said, "Dear father, I don't want
to marry. I am happy here with
my dove." This made her father
angry and he said he would get
rid of her dove.

Prince Florentine had to leave
the castle quickly. So he flew
over the deep, blue sea until he

came to his mother's castle. He asked his mother if she could help, but she said, "I'm sorry, but my magic doesn't reach that far." Instead she told him to go to a more powerful witch called Ostree.

The prince did this, and the powerful witch changed him into a bigger bird. She also sent other large birds to help him. Prince Florentine and the flock of birds flew back across the sea to Earl Mar's castle. They arrived just as his daughter was about to be married to someone else. The birds swooped down and picked up Earl Mar's daughter and carried her back to Prince Florentine's mother.

As they all arrived, the

spell was broken and the prince was no longer a dove. So Prince Florentine, Earl Mar's daughter and their seven sons lived happily ever after.

The Frog Princess

Long ago, it was time for the king's youngest son to marry. The King said, "Shoot this arrow and you will meet your wife where it lands."

But the prince's arrow landed in a swamp beside a frog. Young Prince Ivan was not happy. "How can I marry a frog?" he asked, but the King wouldn't change his mind. So the prince married the frog and they lived in a castle next to the swamp.

The King was getting old and he

271

was thinking about which son to give his palace to. One day he set a test and asked his sons to bring their wives to the palace. Prince Ivan was worried. He didn't want people to laugh at his Frog Princess. But his wife said, "Don't worry, everything will be fine."

That night when the prince went to bed he pretended to fall asleep. He opened one eye and saw his wife take off her frog skin and change into a young lady. She was so beautiful that he fell in love with her at once.

The next morning the prince said nothing to his wife about what he'd seen. He went to the palace alone and saw that his brothers were there with their grand wives. Suddenly, the palace doors opened and the most beautiful princess walked

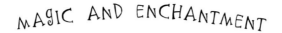

in. Prince Ivan said to the King, "This is my dear Frog Princess."

Prince Ivan felt sure that the king would give his palace to him. To make sure, he ran home and threw his wife's frog skin into the fire. At

274

this there was a clap of thunder and his wife stood before him.

"Why did you burn my frog skin?" she cried. "Now I must leave you forever!" Then she disappeared.

Prince Ivan set off to find his wife. On his way he met an old man who gave him a ball. "Roll this ball and it will show you the way," said the man. Next the prince met a bear, which he was going to kill and eat. But the bear begged the prince to let it live. The prince felt sorry for the bear so he agreed, and they set off together after the ball.

Then a duck flew overhead and the prince took aim with a bow and arrow. But the duck begged the prince to let it live. The prince took pity on the duck too, and set off after the ball with the bear and the duck.

The Frog Princess

After a while the prince and his friends came to a river. A fish leapt out of the water onto the bank. "At last I shall have a

good meal," said the prince. But the fish begged to be thrown back into the water. The prince felt sorry for the fish so he did as it asked.

A little further on, the prince met an old woman. She told him that a witch had taken his wife prisoner and that he must get a special needle to kill the witch and free his wife. This needle was inside an egg that was in a nest on top of a tree.

The prince and his friends set off to look for the tree, which they found quite easily. However, the trunk of the tree was so smooth that when Prince Ivan tried to climb it, he kept slipping down. The bear said "I can help you," and he shook the tree so hard that the nest fell from its branches. But there was a bird sitting on the nest,

and it flew off with the egg grasped in its feet.

Then the duck said, "I can

280

help you," and it flew after the bird. The bird was so scared of the duck that it dropped the egg into the river below. The prince cried, "My wife is lost forever! For how can I get the egg from the river?"

MAGIC AND ENCHANTMENT

Suddenly the fish that the
prince had thrown back into the
river appeared. It had the egg
in its mouth as it swam
to the prince. The
prince quickly
broke the
egg and took
out the needle.
At this, a witch
suddenly appeared, and ran
towards the prince, but he drove

the needle into her heart and killed her. With the witch dead, the spell was broken and the frog princess was free. Prince Ivan went home to find his beautiful wife had returned, and that the King had built them a palace of their own, which was nowhere near the swamp!

The Frog Princess

The Magic Bracelet

There was once a princess called Annabel who was sent to live with her uncle in his castle when her parents died. However her uncle was mean, and he made Annabel live in a

room at the top of a dusty old tower, away from the rest of her family.

Annabel was frightened all on her own at the top of the tower. One night she heard scratching at her door.

Scritch, scratch, scritch.

"Who's there?" said Annabel. There was no answer but she bravely opened the door, and in bounced a friendly, shaggy dog. He leapt on Annabel and licked her face.

"Hello, where did you come from?" laughed Annabel. It was good to have a friend in the lonely tower, and from that night on, the dog, which Annabel called

Toby, stayed by her side.

With Toby to keep her company, Annabel felt brave enough to explore the rest of the tower. Many of the rooms were filled with cobwebs and furniture covered in sheets.

Annabel thought every room was the same, until she opened the last door. This room was beautiful, with a soft carpet, pretty flower curtains and a

dressing table upon
which jewellery
sparkled.

Annabel sat
at the dressing
table and tried
on a glittering
butterfly
brooch, a
heart necklace
and a gold
bracelet. Toby

288

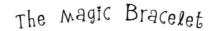

pushed his wet nose against Annabel's leg. He was hungry.

Annabel took off the brooch and the necklace. But when she tried to take off the bracelet it stuck fast, so she left it on.

Annabel often visited the beautiful room. She would sit at the dressing table, trying on the beautiful jewellery. But however hard she tried, she couldn't take off the gold bracelet.

One evening when Annabel was getting into bed, she called Toby, who always slept on her bed with her. But this particular night, Toby didn't come. "Toby, Toby," called Annabel sadly.

But Toby didn't appear the next night, or the night after that. "I wish I could *see* Toby again," sobbed Annabel.

At that moment, the gold bracelet glowed brightly, and

Annabel felt herself flying through the sky. Suddenly she found herself in a garden next to a large cage that was filled with dogs. The dogs had all looked very sad and thin, and Annabel realized they must have been stolen.

"Poor dogs," said Annabel, and she unlocked the cage and set the dogs free. Suddenly, Toby was beside her, barking

joyfully, he was so pleased to
see her.

"I wish we were home, Toby,"
said Annabel as she gave him a

The Magic Bracelet

hug. In
a flash,
the gold
bracelet glowed, and
Annabel and Toby were
back in the tower. Annabel's
uncle was waiting for her, but he
wasn't cross, he was happy to
see her home again. "I was

worried about you," he said.
"Thank you for saving my dog."

Annabel's uncle told her that
Toby was his dog, and that he
let him stay with Annabel
because he knew she needed
company. He was very sorry for
being mean to Annabel, and
invited her to live in the castle
with the rest of the family.

Things were much better
when Annabel and Toby moved

The Magic Bracelet

out of the tower. But Annabel
never told her uncle about the
gold bracelet. Whenever she
wanted to, she would make a
wish, the magic bracelet would
glow, and Annabel and Toby
would go off on an adventure.

Prince Hyacinth and the Dear Little Princess

T here was once a fairy who said to a king, "You will have a son with a big nose, and your son will never be truly happy until he discovers that his nose is big."

Soon after this, the fairy's spell came true. The King did indeed have a son, who was named Prince Hyacinth, and he did have a big nose.

However the King didn't want his son to feel self conscious about his nose. He ordered that only people with big noses were allowed to be in the prince's company, and that no one could say anything about big noses in

front of him.
Because of this, the
prince wasn't the
slightest bit
bothered by
his nose!
One day,
when Prince
Hyacinth was
grown up, his
father said he
should marry.

The prince liked the look of a neighbouring princess called the Dear Little Princess, even though she had a tiny nose, so he paid her a visit and asked her to marry him. But as he bent down to kiss her hand, the princess disappeared. Prince Hyacinth leapt on his horse and went to look for her.

He rode all day, until he came across a cave where a fairy

lived. The fairy and the prince looked at each other and laughed. "What a funny nose!" they both cried. The fairy thought the prince's nose was too big, and the prince thought the fairy's nose was too small.

The prince carried on his search for the princess. But everyone laughed at him. He didn't know why, as he couldn't see that his nose was that big.

Prince Hyacinth and the Dear Little Princess

Then at last the prince found
the Dear Little Princess locked
inside a palace made of glass.
She held her hand out of the
window for the prince to kiss.
But he couldn't reach her, as his
nose got in the way. He cried,
"My nose must be too big!"

At last the prince knew that
he had a big nose! The spell
that the fairy had placed on him
was broken and the glass

palace shattered into pieces. The princess was free, and she married Prince Hyacinth, who was happy at last.

The Firebird

Many years ago, the king's archer was riding through the forest when he found a shining feather on the ground. It was gold and

glittered like a flame. The
archer knew that such a
beautiful feather could only be
from the firebird. So he took
the feather to the king.

But the king was not happy
with just the feather. "A feather
is not a gift for a great king!"
he said. "Bring me the firebird
or I will have you killed!"

In despair, the poor archer
left the king. He didn't know

how he could find the firebird.
But his wise, old horse said,
"Ask the King to scatter a
hundred sacks of seeds over
the fields." So the archer asked
the King and it was done.

The Firebird

The next morning, the archer and his horse hid behind a hedge. Suddenly, there was a gust of wind and a huge golden firebird flew into the field. It dropped down and began to eat the seeds.

The archer crept nearer and nearer. Then, quick as a flash, he leapt on the firebird and tied it up with three strong ropes. He took the firebird to the King.

But the King was still not happy. He locked the firebird in a cage, and this time he said, "Bring me Princess Vassa or I will have you killed!" Again the archer left the King in despair. But his wise horse said to him,

"Ask the king for a golden tent and a selection of delicious food." So the archer asked the king and it was done.

Then the archer set off on his trusty horse. They boarded a ship and sailed across the sea to the faraway land where Princess Vassa lived.

Once he was there, the archer set up the golden tent and laid out all the food. The

tent looked beautiful, and the
young archer invited Princess
Vassa to dine with him.

But the archer had mixed a
sleeping potion in the food. As
soon as the princess took one

bite, she fell asleep. The archer gently placed the princess on his horse and took her to the King.

The King fell in love with the princess and wanted to marry her, but Princess Vassa didn't want to marry the mean King. She didn't tell the King that she had really fallen in love with the kind and gentle archer. So she said, "I will not marry anyone unless I have my wedding dress.

You'll find my wedding dress locked in a big chest in the middle of the sea."

Immediately the king called for the archer. "Bring back that dress, or I will have you killed!" he said. So once more the archer set off on his horse. They came to the sea where the horse spoke to a giant lobster. After a while a great wave crashed on the shore and hundreds of crabs came out of the sea. They carried the chest that had Princess Vassa's wedding dress inside.

The archer took the wedding

dress to the King. He was sad
to do it because he had fallen in
love with the princess. But the
clever princess had a plan. "I
won't marry you until you free
the firebird," she said to
the King. So the
King did just that.
   Then the firebird
swooped down to the princess
and she jumped on its back and
they flew into the sky. The King

The Firebird

ordered the archer to go after the princess, so he leapt on his horse and chased the firebird across the sea to the faraway land where the princess lived. But he didn't bring her back. Instead the archer and Princess Vassa were married, and lived happily ever after.

BEHAVING LIKE A PRINCESS

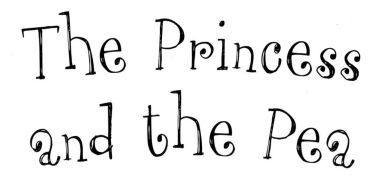

The Princess and the Pea

There was once a prince who wanted to get married. But his future wife had to behave like a real princess.

So the prince travelled all over the world looking for his

princess. He looked everywhere, and visited many different lands. And although he was invited to lots of palaces and met many princesses, he couldn't tell if they were real princesses. There always seemed to be something not quite right about all the young ladies he met.

One evening when the prince was back at home, there was a terrible storm. Thunder crashed and lightning flashed as the rain poured down. Suddenly there was a knock at the palace gates. The old king went to see who was calling at that time of the night.

The king was very surprised to see a princess standing outside. She was wet through, water dripped from her hair and clothes, and her shoes were covered in mud. She didn't look

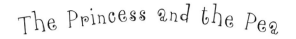

like a princess at all. Yet she told the king that she was!

The king couldn't leave the poor girl standing in the rain. So she was invited in and offered some hot milk and a blanket to keep her warm.

"You may stay the night, my dear," he said.

The queen looked at the girl and didn't think she was a real princess, either. "We shall soon find out," said the queen, and she went away to prepare a room for the girl to sleep in.

The queen went to a guest bedroom and ordered her maids to remove the mattress and all the bed covers from the bed.

The Princess and the Pea

Then the queen placed a tiny pea on the bedstead and instructed the maids to pile twenty mattresses and twenty bed covers on top of the little pea. The bed was so high that it reached the ceiling!

The queen then showed the princess to her room. She gave her some clean night clothes and wished her goodnight. The princess needed a ladder to

climb to the top of the bed!
  In the morning the queen
asked the princess how she had
slept. "Very badly!" said the
princess. And when the
queen asked her why, she
said, "I was kept awake

most of the night by something very hard and lumpy in the bed."

It was clear to the queen that the girl was indeed a real princess. As only a real princess was so delicate

that she could feel a tiny pea through twenty mattresses and twenty bed covers.

So the prince married the real princess. The pea was kept in a glass case in the palace, where it can still be seen today.

The Princess and the Pea

King
Grisly-beard

There was once a King who
had a beautiful daughter.
But the princess was so proud
that not one of the princes who
came to ask her to marry him
was good enough for her.

King Grisly-beard

One day the king invited all the princes who wanted to marry his daughter to a grand feast. But the princess said something mean to every man.

The first man was too fat. "He's as round as a tub," she said. The next man was too tall. "What a tree!" she said. The third man was too short, while the fourth was too pale and the fifth was too red, and so she

330

made a joke about every man.

She also laughed at a king who attended. "His beard is like a mop and he should be called Grisly-beard!" she said. And so the visiting king got the name of King Grisly-beard.

The princess's father was angry at how rude his daughter had been, as these men were their guests. So he said that the princess had to marry the next man who knocked at the palace gate. Two days later a fiddler came knocking and the king invited him in and said he could marry the princess. The princess begged her father to change his mind, but he refused.

So the fiddler and the princess were married. The fiddler led the princess through a wood and she wondered who it belonged to. The fiddler told her

that it belonged to King Grisly-beard, and the princess replied, "If only I had married King Grisly-beard!"

Next the fiddler took the princess through beautiful meadows filled with colourful wildflowers. She asked the fiddler who the meadows belonged to, and again he said they belonged to King Grisly-beard. The princess sighed and

said, "If only I had married King
Grisly-beard!"

Eventually they arrived at a
tiny cottage and the fiddler said
to the princess, "This is your
new home, it is up to you to
keep it clean and tidy." The
unhappy princess also had to do
all the cooking and washing too,
but she wasn't very good at any
of these things.

So the fiddler sent the

BEHAVING LIKE A PRINCESS

princess to the nearest market
to try to sell pots and pans
instead. But she wasn't very
good at that either, and didn't

sell a thing. The fiddler said,
"Perhaps you could try working
in the kitchen at the palace of
King Grisly-beard." So the
princess got a job working as a
maid in the palace kitchens.

After a while the princess
heard that the king was getting
married. This made her sad as
she remembered that she was
really a princess, but she knew
her pride had brought her to

where she was now.

Suddenly, someone walked into the kitchen and turned towards the princess. He asked her to dance with him. The princess realized that it was King Grisly-beard himself. She thought he was making fun of her, and everyone laughed at the princess dressed in maid's clothes. The princess ran to the door, but King Grisly-beard stopped her from leaving.

"I am the fiddler who married you. I pretended to be a fiddler to teach you a lesson about your silly pride."

So the princess was dressed in her most beautiful clothes, and a big feast was held for her and King Grisly-beard, and they lived happily ever after.

The Shepherd's Posy

There was once a King who had a beautiful daughter. A time came when she wanted to get married, so the king invited all the princes of the land to come to the palace to meet the princess. But one prince wanted to see her before all the others did. He disguised himself as a shepherd and set off for the palace, taking some bread to eat along the way.

On the way he met a poor man who asked him for something to eat. So the kind prince gladly gave his bread to the man. The man thanked the prince for his kindness and gave

him three
magic gifts in
return. These
were a spade, a
net and a flute.

When the
prince arrived at
the palace he was
still dressed as a shepherd. He
said his name was Yan and
asked for work, and he was
given the king's sheep to look

after. So he took the sheep to a grassy field, then planted the special spade upright next to the sheep. The sheep would always stay by the magic spade.

Then Yan went in search of a castle that he knew belonged to a giant. "Good afternoon," Yan said to the giant when he found the castle. But the giant wanted to eat Yan for his dinner. As quick as a flash, Yan threw his

magic net over the giant,
who toppled to the ground.
   Then Yan escaped
through the giant's garden,
which was filled with the
most beautiful flowers
that Yan had ever seen.
He stopped to pick some
and made them into a
pretty posy. Yan then returned
to his sheep and played the
magic flute, and the sheep

The Shepherd's Posy

began to dance around him. At that moment, the princess looked out of a palace window and laughed at the dancing sheep. Then the scent of the wonderful posy that Yan had made reached the princess.

"Run down to that shepherd and tell him the princess wants

346

that posy," she said to her
maid. So the maid did.

But Yan wouldn't give the
posy to the maid. He said, "Tell
the princess she must come and
ask for the posy herself. And
that she must say please."

The princess thought the
shepherd was funny. But she
wanted the posy, so she went
down to him and said, "Please
give me that posy." And Yan

gave her the posy.

Every day after that, Yan took some flowers from the giant's garden and made a posy for the princess. And every day the princess stood at the palace

window and waited for him. Each day she said 'please' when she asked for the posy.

The day came when the princess was to meet all the princes. Yan dressed in his finest royal clothes and went to the palace. The princess thought he was handsome but she wasn't sure if he was the shepherd. Before she could speak to Yan, he rode off on his horse. The princess told her guards to stop him, and one grabbed Yan's foot, but he managed to get away.

The princess wanted to find out if the shepherd was really the prince. So she ran to the field where the sheep were grazing. As soon as she saw the shepherd's injured foot she knew he was the prince that her guards had tried to stop. She begged Yan to tell her the truth.

"Please tell me!" said the princess. And because she said 'please' Yan told her that he was really a prince.

The princess was overjoyed, and said that Yan was the prince she wanted to marry. So they were married and lived happily ever after.

The Princess, the Wooden Dress and the Comb

Long ago there was a little princess and her father loved her very much. She was very pretty and loved looking at her face in the glassy waters of pools in the woods. But

sometimes the little princess
was very naughty and her
temper was not as
lovely as her face.
    She would play
in the sand and roll
around in the woods
among the leaves
and bushes
until her curls
were all
tangled up.

353

Her maid combed her hair with a stone comb – for they only had combs made of stone in those days – and she would moan and stamp her foot. When the princess was very angry she would call her maid an elephant! At this, her maid would put her hands up to her face to feel if she had a trunk! One day the princess would rule the land, and the king was worried that his naughty daughter wouldn't grow up to be good and kind.

When the king was out walking in the woods one day, a gentle wind rustled the leaves of an oak tree, and the tree said, "Make a dress out of my branches. When your daughter is naughty, make her wear the dress until she is good."

Next, a huge stag came into the woods. It said to the king,

"Make a comb out of one of my antlers and use it to comb the princess's hair. It will be softer than the stone comb."

So the King had a wooden dress made from the oak tree, and whenever the princess was naughty she had to wear it. The princess didn't like wearing the dress, as it was hard and uncomfortable, and the other children laughed at her. But the dress didn't stop the princess from being naughty.

The King also had a comb made from one of the stag's antlers. And then a strange thing happened. Every time the maid combed the princess's hair with the antler comb, she was sweet and good. She often thanked her maid and said she liked to have her curls smoothed. She even asked to comb her own hair.

In fact, such a change came

over the princess that she didn't wear the wooden dress much after using the comb, and soon she didn't need to wear it at all.

The Unhappy Daffodils

Once upon a time, three daffodils grew under a big, old oak tree. They were fed up and bored and decided they wanted a change. A cuckoo had told the daffodils stories about girls who could run and dance, and the daffodils wished they were girls too. Then one day a fairy heard the daffodils crying, and she asked them why they were so unhappy. The daffodils told the fairy that they wanted to be girls instead of flowers.

"Very well, my dears, you shall be girls," said the fairy. She waved her magic wand over the three daffodils and in a

twinkle they were gone. In their places stood three pretty girls dressed in soft yellow silk dresses and dancing shoes. The daffodils were shocked, but then they laughed and danced happily around the tree.

They thought they were so clever being girls instead of little flowers that no one really noticed. So they set off to see the world. Suddenly they heard a 'cuck-oo' and saw their old friend the cuckoo. He had good news for them.

"The three princes of Silverland are looking for three brides," he said, and the girls

became very excited.

The next day the cuckoo showed the girls the way to the palace. Once they had arrived, the cuckoo told the King that the girls were the Princesses Daffodil from Goldenland. The cuckoo didn't know that there really were three princesses from Goldenland and that they were on their way to the palace. Everyone thought the daffodil

girls were the real
princesses.

They were invited
to a ball where they
danced with the
princes all night.
Everyone said how
beautiful they
looked.

But the next day the real
princesses of Goldenland
arrived at the palace. The

princes couldn't work out who were the real princesses. The only way was to check the girls' feet, as the true princesses had a mark on their big toes. So the princes asked to see all the

princesses' feet to be quite sure who was who. When the princes saw the daffodil girls weren't the real princesses they shouted, "Put them in prison!"

The girls ran from the palace. They ran and ran and ran, not daring to look behind them. Eventually they stopped to rest. And where do you think they were? Why, at their old home under the old oak tree.

The fairy asked, "Well, my dears, do you like being girls?" and there was a twinkle in her eye as she spoke. But the girls were sobbing too much to answer. So the fairy said more kindly, "Will you be happy to be daffodils again?" And they answered, "Yes!"

The fairy waved her magic wand and in a flash the girls were gone and there were three beautiful daffodils growing under the old oak tree once more. From that day on, no cuckoos could tell the daffodils to be anything other than sweet, little daffodils!

The Stubborn Princess

There was once a princess who ate nothing but ice cream. In fact, ever since Princess Uma was a baby she turned her nose up at anything but ice cream.

The Stubborn Princess

The king and queen tried to get her to eat other food but each time they tried, Princess Uma would shout, "Give me some ice cream!" The king and queen didn't know what to do, so they sent out a message to everyone in the land: "We'll give a thousand gold coins to anyone who can get our daughter to eat anything other than ice cream." So people queued up at the palace to try to tempt Princess Uma to eat something else.

First to try was Prince Flatter. He made a delicious casserole with chicken, potatoes, mushrooms and carrots. He dished it up in a gold bowl with a gold spoon and placed it before the princess. But the princess took one look at it and shouted, "Give me some ice cream!" So Prince Flatter quickly left the palace with his casserole.

Next to try was Prince Smooth, who was very clever. He had prepared a scrumptious fruit salad with blueberries, strawberries and bananas, and then he put a dollop of tasty ice cream on the top. But the princess wasn't fooled and she shouted, "Give me only ice cream!" So Prince Smooth also ran out of the palace.

Lastly, Prince Perfect came to the palace, and he presented the princess with a large bowl of... ice cream! Princess Uma greedily ate all the ice cream. Then Prince Perfect gave her some more ice cream, which she also ate. And some more ice cream, and so it went on into the night.

Every time Princess Uma finished eating a bowl of ice

cream, Prince Perfect gave her another bowl. Then at last, when Prince Perfect gave Princess Uma her fourteenth bowl of ice cream, she said, "No more ice cream! I'm sick of ice cream!"

From that day on, Princess Uma never wanted ice cream again. The King and queen gave Prince Perfect a thousand gold coins. And when Princess Uma grew up, she married Prince Perfect and they lived happily ever after.

The Pig Boy

There was once a prince who wanted to marry a certain princess. So he sent her two gifts. The first was a sweet-smelling rose. But when the princess received the rose, she cried, "Ugh!" The second gift was a nightingale, which sang sweetly. But when the princess heard the bird, she cried, "Go away!"

The prince didn't give up. He put on some scruffy clothes to disguise himself, and went to the palace to ask for work. He was given a job as a Pig Boy looking after the king's pigs.

One evening after working all day, the Pig Boy put some bells around a cooking pot. When the pot boiled, it shook the bells and made a tune. The princess was nearby and heard the tune. She wanted that musical pot! So her maid asked the Pig Boy what he wanted in return for his pot. He said, "A kiss from the princess."

The princess wanted the pot

so much that she agreed. She
told her ladies to crowd round
so no one could see. Then she
gave the Pig Boy a kiss.

The next day the Pig Boy
made a rattle that played
music. The princess heard his
rattle and wanted that, too.
Again she told her maid to ask
the Pig Boy what he wanted for
his rattle. This time he said, "I
want two kisses from the

princess." The princess wanted the rattle so much that she agreed. Her ladies stood round her again whilst she kissed the Pig Boy twice. Meanwhile, the king was looking for his daughter. He was shocked to find her

Kissing the Pig Boy, and ordered her to leave the palace.

"If only I had married the prince who sent me the gifts," wailed the princess as she set off alone.

But the Pig Boy ran ahead of her. He hid behind a tree and put on his fine royal clothes. Then he stepped out in front of the princess. "I am that prince," he said to her. "But I don't like you very much now. You were too selfish to see how beautiful a rose smelled or how lovely a nightingale sang. Yet you were happy to kiss a pig boy to get what you wanted."

So the two went their separate ways, and the prince eventually found a princess who appreciated his gifts, and who was thoughtful and kind.